Rabén & Sjögren Stockholm

Translation copyright © 1995 by Rabén & Sjögren
All rights reserved
Originally published in Sweden by Rabén & Sjögren
under the title *Ellens boll*,
pictures and text copyright © 1994 by Catarina Kruusval
Library of Congress catalog card number: 95-067921
Printed in Italy
First edition, 1995

ISBN 91 29 63076 2

Catarina Kruusval

WHERE'S THE BALL?

R&S
BOOKS

Stockholm   New York   London   Adelaide   Toronto

Ellen has gotten a package.

What can it be?

A ball!

Ellen throws the ball high into the air.

And Ellen throws the ball far away.

Then Buster takes the ball...

And he runs off. Buster hides the ball.
The ball is gone!

WHERE IS THE BALL?

Is the ball under the armchair?

Or behind the plant?

Perhaps the ball is on the dresser.

Or in the boots.

Where has Buster hidden the ball?

Perhaps in the box on the sideboard.

No, the ball isn't there.
But there are some cookies.

Buster wants a cookie!

Buster doesn't get a cookie. Buster is dumb.
Buster has hidden Ellen's nice new ball.

Now Ellen is tired.

Ellen is going to take a nap.

But what's under the cover?
It's Buster! And the ball!